FINDING E

A DARK ROMANCE

AMY J. HEART

COPYRIGHT

Finding E: A Dark Romance (Previously titled A Boy Called L) - Damaged Souls Golden Hearts Series Prequel

Copyright © 2018 by Amy J. Heart

Amyjheart.com
amyheartromance@gmail.com

ISBN Paperback: 978-0-6487442-6-9

1

ONCE UPON A NIGHTMARE

Yellow light spills through a crack in the doorway, the color pale and dirty, like the monster who creeps into my bedroom in its wake as if he's made from it or something.

"Go away," I croak, dragging the covers around my shoulders. My bones ache from even that much pressure.

I hum under my breath, trying hard to escape. I need to float away from my body, up to the ceiling, so I can look down at the pale-blue covers that bind me to the mattress as firmly as rope and chains would. I need to see them from afar, not be underneath them, bound and trapped like a trussed-up hog.

The little loser in the bed is nothing to do with me. It's not me. Nope. It's never ever me.

I squeeze my eyes shut and try harder to *leave*, to go somewhere else. Somewhere better. *Anywhere* will do as long as it's out of this room, this bed, this house. But preferably somewhere safer. Wherever Mom is would be perfect.

A sandpaper chuckle breaks through my dry lips. Yeah right. That's impossible—unless I plan on ending things right here and now, so I can join her in the *afterlife*. And I guess I'm an idiot because don't want to do that. Not yet, anyway. Revenge comes first. It has to.

Wrapping my arms tightly around myself, I rock back and forth, the old bed frame squeaking. The sound is soothing. It really shouldn't be.

Wish she was here. Wish she was here. Wish she was here.

Why the hell did you have to go and die on me, Maman? Why?

"You're so skinny, my little lion," she used to say. "I need to fatten you up with lots of treats. From now on, you can have dessert three times a day—buttery cannelés for breakfast, lunch, and dinner."

My fingers, cold but sweaty, fumble under the pillow searching for my most treasured possession, needing to feel its smooth texture, lined with creases from carrying it around in my pocket all the time.

It's a sketch she did of me when I was ten, sitting by the creek, long hair almost touching my bare shoulders, a goofy grin on my dial aimed right at her. I remember every single second of that day like it was yesterday. Sunny and warm, the familiar drone of insects filled the air, and I was happy. Loved. Not alone.

Not like now.

It was *nothing* like now.

The monster in my room right now doesn't care about how skinny I am. Or whether I'm happy or not. All *he* ever says to me is, "Cut your hair, stupid. Are you a boy or what? Or *what*, I reckon." Then he laughs. Gravel on gravel, grinding my bones to dust.

He thinks he's so funny.

But this guy is the farthest thing from amusing I could ever imagine. The polar freaking opposite of a comedian. Yeah, the devil incarnate.

A floorboard near the bed creaks.

"Dégagez!" I yell, choking on rising nausea.

"Speak English, you little shit. Your pretty little French momma ain't here anymore. No one can understand the crap you say."

"I said get out!" My voice echoes in the darkness. Loud. But then the shadows swallow it up immediately. Nobody can hear me.

No one ever hears me.

"That's better. Now I can understand you." He does the gross evil-clown laugh again. "Do I look like some fancy Frenchman to you?"

"No. What you look like is an asshole." I flinch as the sound of leather sliding through denim whips the air. *Whoosh-crack!*

Shit. It's his belt. I shouldn't have opened my dumb mouth. Will I ever learn? Probably not. I may be scared, but I'm always gonna fight back.

"Don't say you didn't ask for it," he says, his voice rough with excitement.

While I wait for the blows to rain down, I tense every muscle, clench my fists so hard they crack. Then it starts. The pain.

I won't cry. I won't scream. It ain't me this is happening to. I'm safe somewhere else. Somewhere far, far away.

I curl into a ball, become as small as I can. I think of my name, reduce myself down to a letter—just one. It's easier this way, if I'm no longer a person. Not a boy. Just one letter.

A letter is nothing, and *no-thing* can take this shit. Because there's no freaking way I can.

"Allez-vous en," I whisper. "Go away." I bite my lip, liquid metal filling my mouth, the taste strangely comforting.

"You're only getting what you deserve, you good for nothing little layabout. I see what a loser you are, boy. I know every shitty thing about you. Hear your every thought. See your every move."

Yeah? Well, here's something he doesn't know about… tomorrow. Tomorrow I turn sixteen, and this year I've promised myself a very special birthday present.

Yep. It's gonna be an awesome gift for me and a fucking brilliant surprise for him. One he'll never see coming.

Because tomorrow, *he'll* be getting what *he* deserves. A gift that all monsters should receive at some point in their shitty, pathetic lives.

A hole blown right through their filthy, flabby, hateful guts.

Yeah. Not long to wait now.

Not long at all.

I crack my eyes open searching for the LED numbers that flash on the bedside clock—it's 12:03.

12:03.

Hot damn! Guess I'm sixteen already.

Happy Freaking Birthday, L.

It's gonna be a good one.

2

———

THE AWESOME FUTURE…OR, YEAH, MAYBE NOT

"**O**h, hell, Lightning, yeah. Yeah!"

I reach up in the dark, wrap my fingers around his neck, and squeeze. I want to make sure it hurts when he comes. His skinny hips buck erratically, revolting dick battering the muscles of my throat. Fingers bury deep in my hair, pulling and tearing. I crush his windpipe tighter and whack his hands away.

"Don't. Touch. Me," I say, slamming him against the restroom wall. He grunts and then makes gurgling sounds. His cock swells, and I taste the first salty drops of come on my tongue. I shove away from him and spit off to the side while semen jets on the concrete between us.

Fucking gross.

Scrubbing my mouth with the back of my hand, I stumble to my feet. The guy's moans and ragged breathing echo off the tiles, making me want to punch him. He looks so stupid,

6

suit pants crumpled at his ankles, a hand rubbing his pudgy stomach in the afterglow.

Afterglow. Now that's wrong. It should be called after-filth. Aftermuck. Aftershit. Any of those would fit the situation better.

The water from the faucet is cold as I rinse my mouth out. Spit. Gulp. Swallow. And repeat.

The creep speaks. "You certainly live up to your name. No wonder you're notorious around the scene. That was damn fast. Incredible and—"

"Shut up. Give me the money."

I stand tall, close, look down at him with my arms folded. The stance draws attention to the size of my biceps, my chest muscles. The tatts curling out of the sleeve of my t-shirt. It says *don't fuck with me.*

He doesn't. He's a lightweight this one. Small. Scrawny. Ugly. And, going by his cultured voice, rich as fuck. He paws his jacket, withdraws his wallet.

"Fifty," I say just in case he's forgotten.

Dark eyes roam my body. "Oh, I think you're worth significantly more than that." He pulls out two Benjamins, and my heart thuds one hard beat. Fuck. I guess this guy is loaded *and* stupid.

He waves the bills between us, then whips them away as I make a grab for them. "Wait on."

Here we go. I'm gonna have to smack him. But, nope, his hand delves back into his wallet and he produces three more bills.

"Because I'm feeling extra generous tonight, here's five

hundred. That absolutely blew my mind, and you're the most gorgeous thing I've ever laid eyes on. I wouldn't want you to starve out there and disappear forever."

I snarl as he puts the money in my palm.

"You swallow next time and I'll double that."

Really? Fuck. This guy *is* an idiot.

Shaking my head, I give him my back and strut to the door.

"See you soon, Lightning," he sing-songs like I'm his pizza delivery guy or something.

Paint flakes off the door frame when I grip it hard, dig my fingernails in deep. "I hope not." I glance over my shoulder and find him still slumped against the bricks. "You might wanna pull your pants up before you leave. You've got nothing to be proud of there."

Shoving the money in my pocket, I walk into the crisp night air.

Hell. Just my luck. It's fucking raining.

3

L'ARBRE

Other than me, there's hardly anyone out hustling in the park. That's weird for a Friday night.

The rain falls harder, but I don't mind. Thanks to the rich idiot who's probably still in the restroom with his pants around his ankles, I'm smiling as I stride along the path in the dark.

My work for the night is done.

And, shit, if I use this money wisely, I might not have to look at another dick for at least a week. Rent is cheap when you sleep under a bridge.

A shiver runs over my skin. Man. It would be heaven to have a break from this hell. Even a short one.

Shame, but I don't think I can do it. I haven't got the resolve, and I want to blow this money faster than I did that dumb suit-guy. I haven't eaten anything since yesterday and stuffing myself full of fucking hamburger isn't gonna satisfy. Neither will gnawing on a cheap hot dog or two. No way.

Tonight, I want something amazing. Mouthwatering and delicious. Like the French stuff Mom used to cook when I was a kid before she went and died on me. Shit, why did my brain have to go there?

The smells of hot butter and Mom's floral skin twist my gut into hard knots. I push away images, sounds—every thought of her—just like I always do. Because remembering anything good about my mom leads to bad thoughts. And memories of *him*.

The wail of a distant siren saves me from downward spiraling thoughts, dragging me back to the here and now. As shitty as it is. But wait—there's that money. I pat the pocket of my jeans to make sure the wad of cash hasn't disintegrated. By some miracle, it's still there.

Chunks of wet, gold hair hang in my eyes. My t-shirt is soaked through, and the rain doesn't look like it'll let up anytime soon. I still don't care. It's beautiful. It smells clean and fresh and normal. And I need some of that last item in my life.

It's what my gut burns for tonight—to feel normal.

Fuck it. I want to feel *better* than normal. Taste something *incredible* instead of gross. Obliterate the tang of a stranger's rank come. Pretend that I'm exactly like everyone else. I want people to look me in the eye without that hint of disgust— like they can't wait to rush away and cleanse me off their retinas, totally unsee me as if I were never there in the first place.

But the reality is that those strangers are right. Being homeless is barely existing.

But, hey, who gives a fuck? I've got five hundred unbelievable bucks getting damp in my jeans right now. I can afford anything I want. Even something special.

Leaves squish under my boots as I cross a barely lit path, taking a shortcut through grass and trees to exit the park fast and get into the restaurant district.

It must be around eight-thirty, so it's busy out. I bump shoulders with Friday night revelers as I stride past Vietnamese cafes, seafood restaurants, strip joints, gin bars, dive bars. Whatever you want to shovel in or guzzle down—you name it—it's all here for your pleasure. I head east, pushing through crowds, until the clothes get fancier, the noses point higher.

Peering in restaurant windows, I try not to sneer at the diners who gawk back at me, looking outraged over their wine glasses.

"Hey, look out!" a gangster-dude says, smacking into me. I stumble sideways because he's a little bigger than me, and that's rare. I might be young but I'm tall, and I spend a lot of time hanging off beams and tree branches to keep strong. Living on the streets, it's best if your appearance says *fuck-with-me-idiot-and-you'll-be-sorry*. Mine blares that sentiment loud and clear.

When I glance up, I spy a gold sign swinging gently from an awning. The way it moves, glinting away in the street lights, is spellbinding.

L'Arbre. Means *The Tree* in French.

Stupid name for a restaurant. Swirling leaves and branches are embossed over the sign. They've entangled me, and I can't look away. I stare for ages as if this is all I need—me and the awesome patterns—nothing else.

But, I *do* need something else. I need to see inside this joint.

Hands stuffed into my pockets, I walk in a daze to the window. The bottom half is covered in gold paint or some weird fabric that keeps the tables, the layout, and the customers hidden. It's a French grill restaurant and going by what I can see of the ceiling—again covered in gold—it's swanky as fuck. Upscale. Out of my league. And I want inside so bad it hurts.

Mouth twisting, I inspect my duds. The Nirvana t-shirt I stole yesterday is kinda clean. My jeans with the knees ripped out, not so much. I earned every tear in them, too, and not in a cool way. My black boots have gaffer taped soles. Shit. I look exactly like what I am. A hobo.

My stomach groans loudly. I need to get inside this place and fill my gut up. But I hesitate, reluctant to make an ass out of myself. They'll probably kick me back into the gutter.

What will I lose if I try? Only my dignity and that's long gone. If they call the cops, I can run fast. So fuck it, I'm going in. I tuck my hair behind my ears in a pathetic attempt to increase my respectability and open the door.

Ah, hell! Why did I do that?

I've stepped into a dream. One of those nightmares where you turn up to school dressed in chaps and a dumb hat, and it turns out wild-frontier day isn't until next week. Or you're like… completely naked at a funeral.

The cavernous space drips with gold and, fuck, it's loud. Classical music plays, but it's the good type. Full of warmth and life. There are suits everywhere, ladies in slinky dresses, and a sea of shiny up-dos floating above swanlike necks.

A beautiful blond girl slithers out from behind a metallic desk, velvety, red dress shimmering over her thighs as she glides toward me. She's smiling, but it looks a little strained.

"Good evening, sir." She tips her head regally and glances down at her copper clipboard. Like the sign out the front, it has leaves and branches engraved in the metal. "May I have the name of your booking, please?"

My heart thuds so loudly I'm amazed she doesn't start tapping her pen along with the beat. I clear my throat to drown it out. "Ah, I don't have one."

Smiling politely, she scans my body then bounces her gaze around my face. "And the number in your party this evening?"

"What?"

"How many people will be joining you?"

Shit. I should at least talk like my brain works. I can do a lot better. I don't spend days in libraries reading shit, trying to keep stuff in my head for nothing. I've been out of school now thirteen months, and I miss it like hell.

"Uh, it's just me." *Man.* No great improvement there.

"A table for one, then, sir. I'll just confirm we can accommodate you. Please wait there." She slinks off behind a long bar tucked against the wall and consults with a man. He's

Don Draper smooth with teeth so white you crave sunglasses when he opens his mouth.

Don ducks his slick head around a metal column and checks me out while flashing those blinding whites. It's a smile I know well. Translated it means this... *you're doing something to my favorite organ, the one that lives in my pants, and I like it a lot.* But not me, I don't enjoy it one bit. That smile makes me feel bad.

He gives the girl a nod, and she weaves her way through the surreal setting toward me. Feeling like I'm watching a movie, I hold my breath.

"We have a lovely table for you tonight, sir. I'm sure you'll be very pleased with it."

I'm pretty fucking sure I will be, too.

I nod. "Great."

"Please follow me."

Thank fuck. I'm about to faint from hunger. The food smells are pure torture.

I squelch my way through the restaurant, hoping my socks dry out soon.

A long table flows down the center of the room, smaller ones scattered on either side. They're overflowing with flowers and food and surrounded by chattering rich folk. A massive mural adorns the back wall, kinda biblical but sexy. Gold drips like stalactites from the ceiling. Seems like I've time-traveled to an old European palace.

Sleek heads follow my bedraggled progress. I must look hilarious, dressed for a rock concert while their attire is all *Night at the Opera.*

The girl stops at a table for two that has a perfect view of the whole joint. I'm stunned they haven't shoved me out of sight. The white linen is so neat and clean with way too many utensils laid out in a complicated arrangement. I have no clue what to do with most of them. But, hey, tonight I don't give a fuck.

"Will this be satisfactory?" she asks, patting her perfect hair.

I grin like a kid. I can't help myself. "Fuck, yeah… ah, I mean absolutely."

She giggles. Not something you normally hear from an ice queen. Guess I'm a funny guy.

"Where's the bathroom? I came off my bike on the way here," I lie. "And now I need to, you know, freshen up a little."

She gives directions, and I enter the most amazing restroom I'm sure I'll ever live to see.

Man, these people love their gold. It's everywhere. And other than that, it's all black tiles and mirrors. Too many mirrors. Everywhere I look, there's me reflected back and, right now, I don't need reminding of what I look like. No thanks.

The central chandelier is about the size of a baby elephant. It sprays rainbow prisms over the silver and gold wallpaper and my clothes. *Cool.* It's an improvement to my shitty appearance, but it makes me dizzy.

I take a piss and then, ignoring the mirrors, make friends with the soap. I splash water on my skin, comb wet fingers through my hair, and scrub my face. Fluffy hand towels hang from copper rails. As I press a cream-colored one against my cheek, longing seeps into my chest—for what, I'm not sure.

While I dry off as best as I can, I sniff my armpits and a laugh bursts out. Shit, I smell like fucking soap. I'm mostly clean! And I love it.

After that, I stare at my reflection like an imbecile. I'm shocked. I don't recognize myself. The guy gazing back at me looks crazy, desperate, and as mean as all the other assholes I meet living rough out there.

Stares from diners burn holes through me as I trek back to the table. Fuck these people snickering and whispering to each other. I don't care what they think.

Cutlery clatters as I take a seat and grin at the girl who hands me a fancy, fabric-covered menu with one hand and hides that thawing-ice-queen giggle with the other. Probably laughing at my wet hair.

Biting my lip, I check out what's on offer. It's all in French. And, of course, I can understand it. Not everything, mind, but quite a lot. It makes my chest hot. I want my mom.

What? That's fucking ridiculous. Am I eleven or something? I push back memories. Sounds. Soft touches. Quiet words. French nursery rhymes. Shit. What am I doing in this place? It's bad for my health.

"Shall I suggest something, sir?"

"What? No, thanks. I can read it," I say, frowning.

Of all the posh places in the area, trust me to pick a French one. "I'll have the Côte de Bœuf Grillée," I say in a perfect Toulouse accent. Thanks, Mom. Fuck, but it hurts to hear that sound come out of my mouth. I slap the menu on the table so I can't see the words anymore.

The girl, whose name tag says *Sandrine*, has a proper smile for me now. Like she's decided that if I can speak French, I must be some kinda bad-boy billionaire. A potential date. She wouldn't be looking at me like that if she knew what I'd been doing on my knees an hour ago.

"And uh… could I have a beer please? You choose one for me."

She bats her eyelashes. "What attracts you in a beer?" The way she's licking her red lips makes me think that she's not talking about beverages.

"Something fresh. Clean tasting."

"Coming right up," she purrs, and swings her svelte hips away. She's pretty sexy. If I was normal. If I wasn't fucked up, I'd definitely want to tap that.

There's nothing to do while I wait other than listen to my stomach moan. I don't even have a cell I can pull out and pretend to scroll through texts as though I have a life. Like I've got family or friends. Or anyone who gives a shit.

So I kick back and discreetly sniff the insanely great food smells, eavesdropping on snippets of conversation. Then my beer arrives. Don Draper serves me this time. Bubbly amber liquid gets poured into a glass, and the guy flirts his ass off with me while looking over his shoulder every few seconds at the girl behind the bar.

They've got some kind of game going on that involves me. Maybe to see who can discover the most about the weird street urchin who's made it through the palace gates. Or maybe they'd like me to fuck them in turn against some dumpsters out in the back lane. But whatever it is they're hoping for, I ain't biting. I'm polite, but I want this guy to go away so I can enjoy my normal—no, my *special*—time in peace. Even if it is only for an hour.

The beer gives me something to do with my hands. It's icy and goes straight to my head courtesy of my empty stomach. The buzz makes me careless, and as I check out an elegant old broad's meal, I accidentally lock eyes with her.

The plate sizes look decent. Thank fuck. I'd probably cry if they were bird-sized.

This woman is interesting. Middle-aged, very classy, and I guess the best word to describe her face is handsome. She raises a regal eyebrow and one side of her scarlet lips at me. I give her a nod, ignoring the silver foxes in sharp suits at her side.

Better not look her way again. Don't wanna give her any ideas.

Shit, I can feel her staring as I drink my beer, play with my knife, then a dessert spoon. I won't look. I won't look.

Finally, my meal arrives. Ribs. I nearly black out from the impact of the juicy, fatty smell. The hot, spicy sizzle. Before the ice queen has even left the table, I'm hunkered over my plate, attacking the meat like an animal. I *am* an animal, and I don't give a shit if I look uncivilized.

All my senses narrow to the meat in front of me, focus, and I just *feel* and *breathe* the meal down in greedy mouthfuls. Christ, it's unreal.

In under five minutes, I've used a whole basketful of

bread and soaked up every orgasmic drop on the white plate. I'm exhausted. This must be what good sex feels like for normal people. Transporting. Base, savage, and the best thing ever.

When I lean back, my chair creaks. I don't realize I've closed my eyes until I hear a raspy, cultured voice above me.

"You enjoyed that, darling?"

My eyes fly open. It's the attractive old broad. "Fuck, yeah. Yes, *ma'am*, I did." I drag the title out in a sarcastic drawl.

I wonder how much dough she'll offer me to eat *her* out for dessert.

"Can I join you?"

Here we go.

"Sure. Why not."

She sinks into the chair, crossing her well-toned legs gracefully. "My dinner guests and I were watching you."

The two swish dudes lift their glasses at us.

"No kidding."

She plays with a sapphire pendant that sparkles between her breasts. It's probably real. Not sure about her breasts, though. Shit, she's so noble looking I can't even *think* the word tits when I'm sitting this close to her.

"You're an incredibly beautiful young man."

"Really? Huh. Thanks, I guess."

"I imagine you've heard that a lot."

I nod. I sure fucking have.

"Let me buy you a drink. What do you fancy? Top shelf

whiskey? Or we could split a bottle of the most expensive champagne *L'Arbre* has to offer."

"You could afford that?"

"Yes, of course."

Shit. "I'll just have another beer."

"You're young."

I nod.

"No more than twenty?"

"Almost nineteen."

"That young. And what is your name?"

I don't want to tell her. No, maybe I do. It'll be fun to watch her expression change and grow scornful.

"Lightning."

She smiles but doesn't give me the satisfaction of looking shocked. "You have very, *very* blue eyes. And so beautifully shaped. Do you wear colored contacts?"

Jesus. I laugh. "No. They're my real eyes."

She calls the waitress over. Orders drinks in an arrogant manner.

Licking her glossy lips, she shakes her head at me. "Your beauty is utterly devastating. Your face. The bone structure. Your body. Perfectly packaged raw, male sex appeal. A tattooed avenging angel. You are exactly what I need."

I'm sure I am. And she's right about the avenging part.

I lean in and give her a blast of the electric eyes she's so into. "You know, lady, this is getting boring. I reckon your friends over there must be missing you by now."

"I see this toughness you exude is no act." She smiles and reaches into a black and gold purse. It goes nicely with the decor. "But I think your bark is worse than your bite. Otherwise I would not be so drawn to you." She pushes a card across the table. Who uses business cards these days?

I check out both impressive sides. Ariana Wilde. Really?

"I'm an agent for one of the most prestigious modeling agencies in both Europe and America. I can procure you a tremendous amount of work, Lightning." She pauses and pats my hand. "And I can make you very rich."

I kinda choke a little on my beer. That's not what I was expecting her to say. "Bullshit."

"I would not lie to you. It is the truth. So, tell me about yourself. What do you currently do, Lightning?"

"Most people call me L."

"Alright, then—L it is." Her smile grows. "The clients will love that. It suits you. Wonderfully direct and sexy. So you're a struggling artist? A musician?"

"Wrong, but sorta close. I live under a bridge and suck dirtbags off so I can buy a burger and fries every few days. And I try not to die of starvation. So, yeah, you were right. I'm a pretty creative guy."

This time her face *does* change, her expression turning my blood piping hot.

I fucking hate pity.

"So how much are you thinking of offering me to fuck you? Have you got a car parked nearby? You probably wouldn't wanna take me back to your home. That'd be dangerous. I should mention that as a bonus I give great head. In fact, I'm famous for it." I don't tell her that I have zero experience doing it to a female. "That's how I got my name… Lightning… because I'm real quick at—"

"Shhh." She puts a soft hand over mine. "L, please stop. Be quiet and I will make a call to a friend. This man works for my agency, as I hope you will soon. Together, he and I will help you."

I don't understand what she means. Help me? People don't do that for nothing.

"My friend can answer all your questions concerning this work I spoke of. Now relax. I promise you will not have to do those horrible things ever again."

While she taps on her phone, I can't stop swallowing. There's a lump about the size of a packet of smokes in my throat that won't shift no matter what I do.

When she holds the cell up to her ear—it's gold, of course —a wide smile brightens her face, making her look trustworthy. "Angelo, darling! Yes, of *course* it's me. How many other Arianas do you know, sweetie? Oh, three others!" She tinkles out a laugh. "Well, then. It seems I must change my name to a more remarkable one!"

She's still wearing her kind face. But I'm not stupid. No one's honest or dependable. No matter how nicely they smile, they all want things from you. Bad things. Wrong things. And then cry and shout and blame you for making them want that stuff in the first place.

"So, darling, how was Tokyo? Mm hmm… that sounds wonderful. I want to hear all about it, but for now I need to speak with you about a favor. His name is Lightning—" She breaks off to laugh again. "Yes, *Lightning,* that's what I said.

I'm hoping he'll come to work for me, but he has nowhere to stay. Wait until you see him, he's the most beautiful waif."

Light glints off her jewelry as she scans me from head to toe.

"Yes, that's right. He's my new project. Can you look after Lightning for me until we get him on his feet? The two of you will be great friends. I promise." She smiles and nods and trills like a fucking parakeet. "Thank you, darling. You truly are an angel. Love you." She makes kissy noises and ends the call.

She's beaming at me.

"Who the hell was that?"

"My Angelo. You will love him."

Probably not in the way she's imagining.

"No, don't scowl at me, L." Her graceful hand shoots out. "Pass me your cell instead."

I don't move.

"No phone?" She sighs and tut tuts at me. "I'll send a wonderful one over to you in the morning. You're going to need it."

"Over to where?"

"To Angelo's, of course, silly." She pulls out a sparkling pen—probably diamond encrusted—and scrawls on a napkin. "Here. Go to his apartment and stay there. Be warm. Be safe. Have fun. And let me fix your life for you."

I frown. "So… you don't want me to fuck you tonight?"

Grinning like a pixie, her gaze sweeps over me. "L, what I want and what I actually *do* day to day, or night to night in your case, are two very different things. I'm going to help you, not take advantage of you."

There's that word again. Help. Yeah, right.

"And make us both lots of money while I do so."

Bingo. There it is. The truth.

She summons a waitress, demands a triple serving of crème brûlée in one bowl, and tries to extract information from me while I attack the sickly-caramel goodness. In six seconds, I've inhaled the lot.

I give her zilch details about my past, sweet fuck all about my current situation, and, still, she pays for my food and gives me a hundred-dollar bill for travel expenses.

As I get to my feet, all eyes in the room shift my way. Fucking busybodies.

"Now, you'll go straight to Angelo's apartment, L darling, won't you?"

I nod. "Sure."

"Because I wouldn't want to lose you. Not when I've only just found you."

I laugh as I stuff the money and the napkin with the address on it in my pocket. It's kinda funny to have someone care about what I do—even if they *are* only pretending.

Thin limbs shoot up, balancing on towering heels, and she steps around the table like a racehorse heading for the feed bin. "This is not a joke, L. It is real. I want you to think of me as your personal fairy godmother come to grant your every wish."

Okay, sure thing, crazy woman.

One corner of my mouth hikes into a smile.

Her jewel-covered fingers clutch my t-shirt, pulling me closer, and then her arms wrap around my neck. She's fucking hugging me! Shit. No one's tried to do this since Mom died.

My hands hang limp, heart dancing against my ribs.

I want to drop to the floor. I want to push her away.

My palm lifts, then falls. Then lifts again until it's resting against her back. This is insane. I'm touching someone and, as far as I can tell, there's nothing at stake here. Nothing to sell. No sex-vibe. Nothing. It's sleaze-free, as if she only wants to comfort me.

Two light kisses tickle my face. Then she strokes my cheek, and says, "Trust me."

Guess I'll give it a go. Like I said before, I've got nothing to lose.

Whispers swirl as I sway through the tables, heading for the exit. It's hard not to listen to the shit people splash around.

The popular opinion is that I'm an up-and-coming actor. But some think I front a happening rock band and that Ariana is my manager. Huh. That's cool. A few people bravely snap pics as I pass. It's all very hilarious.

If I wasn't freaking out, I'd be doubled over laughing.

4

THE GIRL

I stagger out of the restaurant holding my aching stomach. Overindulging hurts like hell. And it feels fucking amazing.

It's nearly eleven, and I'm so giddy from the idea that I might actually be warm tonight, might sleep on something soft, that the pavement rolls like an earthquake beneath my boots. Shit, there's a chance that maybe for the first time in like… months, I'll be safe.

Months? No, that's wrong. If I include the period of my fucked-up childhood, it's more like years since I've gone to sleep without fearing for my life. An age since I've drifted off in peace.

I should find a cab and head straight over to this Angelo guy's place, like Ariana suggested. But I can't. My head is too messed up, spinning with the unbelievable events of the last couple of hours. I need to wander downtown for a while and process the fuck out of it. Because, somehow, within a very short space of time, I went from kneeling in a stinking restroom to lounging back in princely luxury.

Fucking crazy.

It started out exactly the same as every other shitty night I spent cruising for money to stay alive for a few more days.

Head pounding. Tick.

Gut nauseous. Yep.

Sucked a guy off. Check.

Hated myself for doing it. Oh, yeah.

Contemplated walking in front of a speeding car to end the misery. Roger that.

And then…

Dined at a palace. Got ogled by an ice queen, Don Draper, and my fairy godmother all within the same hour.

Wait a second… back the fuck up.

Maybe if I shake my head hard enough, I'll wake and find that I'm back under the bridge—home sweet fucking home— while old Nelson steals my rotting blanket, the prodding of his bony fingers conjuring dreams of classy broads and walls that drip with gold.

I stop dead in my tracks, and a guy crashes into me. "Move!" he says, circling around.

What is it with these people? "Sorry, man."

Weaving unsteadily in his classy duds, he looks over his drunk-as-fuck shoulder. Dark eyebrows jump, and he zips around, walking backward to check me out. His eyes sleaze their way down my body. I curl my lip at him and not in a friendly way. On any other night I'd have forced a crooked smile and a head flick. The universal signal for *you got the money - I've got the time.*

The guy takes a step forward and I growl like a freaking werewolf. Giving me the finger, he turns and disappears into the mob of people. There goes an easy fifty bucks.

But, tonight, thanks to Ariana's fairy godmother wand, I don't think I need to give any fucks at all.

What I do need—is to see that business card again, make sure I didn't imagine it.

"Come on. Come on," I mutter, fumbling in my front pocket. With my luck, it's probably slipped through a tear in the denim. Wait. I remember shoving it in the back pocket. Yep. I can feel the cardboard. Thick and smooth.

Finally, I tug it out. Thank fuck. It's as real as the pavement cracks I've been tripping over, the letters, glossy raised bumps under my fingernails. I can't stop rubbing them. They're gold. What a surprise.

I stare at her name glowing in the light of an amber neon sign.

Ariana Wilde.

Ariana Wilde.

That lady is the most elegant thing I've ever seen. So confident. And probably full of shit.

More than anything, I want this woman to be on the level, but given the way my clusterfuck of a life has gone so far, it's unlikely. But the only way to know for sure is to knock on this dude's door. And if he turns out to be any sicker than the restroom-guys, I can always pummel the crap out of him.

I drag numb fingers through my hair and frown at the

crowds stumbling in and out of cafes and bars. These people have jobs. Friends. Normal lives. And somewhere warm to sleep every single night.

I try not to let jealousy crush me, because it sure as fuck won't do me any good.

The rain continues to piss down, wind tearing through my cotton t-shirt. Shivering, I realize I need to steal a coat pretty soon, because the weather's already turning brutal. Better do it tomorrow.

But maybe I won't need to if Angelo and his spare bed end up being real and Ariana can magic me up some paid work for…

For getting my photo taken?

Yeah, right.

With my luck, I'll be the star of a snuff film and get my limbs hacked off in some dingy basement. I can just hear this Angelo dude when he's done with me…

Here, L. Here are your thousands of dollars for your super hard work. Um… hello, Lightning? You awake? Oh, you're dead? Shit. Sorry about that. Since you'll have no use for this money now, I guess we'll just reinvest it in our next exciting film.

Ah, well, I suppose that'd be one way to end the misery that is my dismal life. But there are probably less painful ways.

Shoving the card deep in my pocket, I study the street, musing on what I should do next. Back to the bridge to attempt some shut eye? Or off to the potential serial killer's pad? Great freaken choice!

I decide to head for the seedy part of town—where I

belong—so I can remind myself of the garbage I might actually leave behind if I have the balls to take a gamble on Ariana and her promises.

Who the hell am I kidding? I want that warm place to sleep tonight more than I want to score. I'll be rolling the dice for sure.

Drugs. Now that's a fucked-up scene. I try not to buy too often, the streets are hard enough without an addiction to feed, but getting high blurs the edges nicely, makes everything butter soft for a few hours. And shuts off the nightmare voice inside my head.

It's a filthy way to live—like an animal really—but I'm as human as those rich fuckers back there in the ritzy district. I deserve a chance at a better life.

After ten minutes of walking in a stupor, I'm back among the grunge, the strip clubs, and hookers.

Standing on Jackson with my hair dripping water down my back, I stare at the drug dealers and shitty burger joints. The sight of Joe Junior's in particular churns my gut. After the last meal I ate there, I puked for two days straight. That was a fun time to be homeless.

The rain-drenched street is like a movie set—a glistening, weird sci-fi porno film or something. To kill time I check the people out, casting them roles in the movie I'm making in my head.

The old guy huddling in the hardware store doorway, trench coat ragged, is a mad scientist on the run from a genetics lab. A yard away from him stands a girl in a black dress. She's the love interest or…

What. The. Fuck.

I do a double, triple fucking take back to her.

"My. God."

Huh? Did I just say that out loud?

I've never before even *thought* the words *my god*. Growing up under the same roof as a real-life demon, there's never been any point in appealing to a higher power. Or enthusing like a sixteen-year-old to one. Any second now I might start bouncing on my toes and squealing like a cheerleader.

Worse. What the fuck is my body doing? I feel hot, itchy. Turned on.

Who the hell is this girl? And why does my dick care?

Okay, idiot. Chill out.

I need to use my head—the one between my shoulders would probably work best—and stop freaking out. Calm down and look at her again. She's just a girl.

So I gulp back some air and then look.

Everything around her warps, sliding into slow motion, like that Munch painting—The Scream—I saw in an art book at the library a while ago. Colors stretch and go fuzzy. Street noises disappear. This must be a dream, most likely a nightmare, but it's too early to tell yet.

So this girl, she's kinda small. The black dress she's wearing is skin tight, short, and not nearly warm enough. I can tell because she's rubbing her arms trying to warm up. Long hair—possibly brown—hangs over her tits. And far out… the rack on her is just… *spectacular*. Big. Too big for her tiny waist, but the incredible curve of her hips balances them out, turning her into an hourglass. A wet dream. A goddess.

My chest aches like I've been shot straight through the ribcage with a metal rod or something. Despite eating enough crème brûlée to fill a beer keg half an hour ago, my gut feels hollow.

Two words ram my brain over and over, stunning me stupid.

I. Want.

I. Want.

That's all I can think, like I'm a kid gawking in a shop window at a whiz bang toy, knowing there's no way I'll get it for fucking Christmas.

But why this dumb longing? This powerful need.

To be close.

To touch.

And, unbelievably, when I look at this girl, I forget that sex means fear and pain. I can't hear that voice—the one that lurks in the dark, taunting me from the past—from that long-ago bedroom. For me, sex equals *only* that voice. But at this moment, I can't hear it. And even if I could, I'd just tell it to shut the fuck up.

Because I want her.

I want her in *that* way.

A laugh rumbles out of me, because that's a stupid idea. I don't ever want any one in *that* way. Never have. Never will. Well, except that right now, there's no denying the heat-party starting in my jeans or the fact that I do—I *do* want her.

I want to fuck her.

This is all so ridiculous, because I wouldn't know what to do with her even if I did get ahold of her—really wouldn't have a fucking clue how to proceed. I've never touched a girl before. Never wanted to. Well, maybe I've wanted to a *little*. I've definitely looked before, checked out some hot curves. Some inspiring butts. And wondered.

But I keep my distance from the girls on the streets that stare at me. Even the ones that live hard—live rough—like me. And then there's the college girls. The business chicks. I don't want to scare them. They don't deserve my anger. My pain. My filth. No way. And, plus, I've never wanted any of them enough to try… to see what would happen if I *did* touch them.

This girl in the black dress, for some bizarre reason, she's different.

I want to know what she feels like.

Tastes like.

Sounds like.

I *need* to know.

Is her skin smooth? Soft? What color are her sad eyes? Would she care that my hair is dirty? My skin? My soul.

What would it be like to kiss her? Press my lips against hers, and then fuck her mouth with my tongue. Not that I would know how to do that. I've only had guys try to do that to *me*. Kiss me. Then I fuck *their* mouths with my fist.

So, this girl would have to show me everything, guide me. I wonder if she would?

Jogging on the spot to keep warm, she looks across the street. If I don't move, in half a breath she'll look right at me. I'm not ready for that just yet, so I duck into the shadows. I'm not close, but I'm near enough to be assaulted by her eyes. Wow. I've never seen such a sad face before.

My heart pounds. What will happen if I step out from the darkness and go and speak to her?

I could say something like… 'Hey, my name's Lightning. What's yours?' and then vomit crème brûlée all over her high-heeled boots. No. I don't reckon I'd puke on her. I've faced scarier things. I mean, I would only talk to her. It's not like I can ask her on a date. Not in my situation. But maybe… maybe if things work out with this Ariana…

I don't know what to do. I can't decide.

Would a girl like her give a guy like me her cell number? I could call her tomorrow on the one Ariana is supposedly sending over. My brain whirs uselessly. I could show myself and risk scaring the crap out of her or walk away and maybe regret it forever. Guess I should… Wait—she's with someone?

She turns toward Joe Junior's, smiling as an older guy steps through the doorway and passes her a bag of grease.

My brain screeches to a halt. Jesus mother-freaking hell. Talk about a sucker punch. I lose control of my limbs, my stomach, and the crème brûlée lurches up and sprays over the concrete.

Fuck.

That guy standing next to black-dress girl is Cooper.

Cooper!

What the fuck is it with this goddamn stupid night?

I'm dumbstruck. Feverish. It's been years since I've laid eyes on him, and all I can see is red fucking blood and black fucking murder.

Hate.

I'm shimmering, blistering wrath and I'm gonna kill that fucker. I swear it.

He's not the first prick to fuck me over. Things had gone to shit long before I met him, but a couple of years ago, Cooper was first on the scene when I most needed help. And the dirty-slob-cop that he was, he chose to wrap me in chains, torture the fuck out of me, and drive nails into my coffin.

My shock morphs into a rage that fires through every cell, even my fucking hair is fuming. I wipe my mouth and picture several ways to cause him pain. Somehow, I stop myself from rushing over to get started on him.

Because with Coop's connections, if he sees me, I'm a dead man. For me to finish him, it'll need to be an ambush—a surprise attack. So I stay put.

Why is he with this girl? Why *her*?

I shake while I watch them eat fries and talk. She makes him laugh, but every time he looks away, her eyes turn haunted. She's beautiful, but in a tragic way. It distracts me from hating on Coop. Maybe it's her sadness that calls to me. But I can't believe she's associated with that dirtbag—the filthy ex-cop who holds my soul to ransom.

What an insane night. I feel worse than I did at the beginning when I was starving.

The rain has soaked through my top, and it clings to my chest in a suffocating way. I tip my head back and open my mouth, icy water splattering my tongue. It feels good. Cleansing. So, that's it then. I'm outta here.

Good fucking riddance sad-girl. And Coop.

For now.

Walking fast, I head in the opposite direction. I need to get maximum space between my past and my future asap.

When I've stomped about two blocks, I hail a cab and give over Ariana's friend's address.

Enveloped in the heater's warmth, I drop my head back against the seat and let my mind wander. Immediately, it snaps back to the girl. Even after seeing her with Coop, I still want to speak to her, get her name. Ask if I can follow her to wherever the fuck she's going just so I can look at her. And dream about touching her.

Jesus, what is this shit? It's pathetic.

And then I let myself think about *him*.

That asshole Coop.

The Coop-factor must have caused my bizarre reaction to the girl. I could probably sense him on her—all the stress and hate and anger and pain that goes along with that guy. It's got me all revved up. On edge. Ready to fight. Or *fuck*. Because that's a weird thing about the fight or flight instinct. When it kicks in, you want to kill someone or fuck something.

I guess.

Half an hour later, the cab slows in front of a multi-story apartment complex, one of those renovated warehouses. In fact, the street is full of them. This is the industrial zone behind the beach—a cool area. There's even an art gallery next door and a cafe that has slabs of wood for outdoor tables and wine barrel seats.

It's a promising sign. And the kind of place you could bring a girl like sad-eyes home to.

Well, I shouldn't get too excited just yet. Even hipsters can be psychopaths.

"Thanks, man," I say to the driver as I hand him the hundred bucks. "Keep the change." Might as well spread the good fortune around, and if I get whacked tonight, I won't be needing money.

Loud rock music wafts down from a window. Party sounds. Laughter.

More good omens.

Just in case it's my last opportunity to star-gaze, I give the sky a long look. It's too cloudy for any real satisfaction.

Man, in my line of work, it's dumb to rock up to a stranger's house. Within the hour, I might be minced into sausage filling.

Fuck it. Here goes nothing. Before I can change my mind, I bolt up the steps and press the intercom.

5
———

ANGELO

"Lightning? Is that your ass out there?"

I leap out of my skin at the loud voice crackling through the intercom. "Yeah. It's me."

"Don't just kill time on my doorstep, man. What are you waiting for?"

"I'm waiting for your maid to buzz me in. *You fuckwit.*" I say the last bit under my breath. No need to get him offside. There'll be plenty of time for that later on.

He laughs, the noise like rumbling thunder. Then a long beep sounds. "At your own risk, ride the Starship Enterprise up to the top floor. Mine is the green door at the end."

Because I'm a smartass, I say, "Yes, sir," and then open the steel doors.

My jaw hovers an inch off the floor as I take in the massive foyer. It has a pressed tin ceiling that hangs high like stars, the space between the walls so cavernous you could

38

run a nightclub in it. There's blond wood, exposed brick, and metal everywhere. It's shiny. Sharp. And cool as hell.

There's no doubt in my mind that this Angelo guy makes big bucks. Which is reassuring. I *think*. I still might be plunging deeper into the shit with Ariana and her so called *friend*, but I guess there's only one way to find out. And that involves committing to the elevator.

Angelo wasn't kidding about it. Inside the bling-filled gizmo, it's full-on Star Trek. In five heartbeats, it propels me up ten floors. And, ah, more fucking mirrors. Again, I'm surrounded by them. I look bad. Slumped shoulders. Beaten up clothes. Pissed as all get-out.

Happy to be removed from the sight of myself, I cruise down an eerily lit hallway, beams of light crisscrossing over my skin. This whole place gives off a serious Blade Runner vibe.

When I arrive at the green entrance, I knock twice. *Please, please.*

I'm not sure what I'm silently begging for, but it sure as fuck isn't the sight that greets me when the door swings open. Because *Jesus Christ*, I'm staring at a Nubian princess crossed with a rasta dude.

With shoulder length dreads, bulging muscles covered in dark mocha skin, eyelashes as long as a giraffe's—this guy is the prettiest freaking thing I've ever seen.

Doe eyes wide, his pouty lips say nothing.

"You Angelo?" I ask.

He flinches like he's amazed I can speak. "Shit, man, I'll be anything you want me to be!" He grins and yanks me into his apartment by my t-shirt. Scratching his chin, he circles me like a shark while I give him my best piranha smile. He better not fucking touch me again.

He gives a long whistle. "*Damn*, boy, you are really something else. No wonder Ariana sounded like she was shitting bullion on the phone. *Lightning Boy*. Fuck! Pretty as a pony and as hard as a muscled-up gangsta rapper. Ka-ching, ka-ching. You's the shit boy."

I narrow my eyes and puff my chest out a bit. "*Boy?* How the fuck old are *you?*"

"Twenty. Relax, man. I don't bite. Come. Come on over here and sit." He ushers me onto a king-sized couch and retreats to a high-tech kitchen. "Want a beer?"

"Yeah, sure." Might be my last. Or maybe not. This jerkoff isn't exactly giving off serial killer vibes.

I try to keep my mouth closed while I check out his digs but fail miserably. *Shit!* Tonight, it seems all I've done is travel from one incredible movie set to the next.

Exposed brick columns, humongous wooden beams, stupid sized windows, a fireplace I could live in, and the largest flat screen TV that's surely ever been sold leave me gob smacked.

"It's cool, huh?" he says, handing me a beer as he reclines opposite. He nods at the screen. "You like gaming?"

"Uh, probably. Never tried it, but I'm sure it's a good time."

"You never gamed? Shit. You're a babe-in-the-woods, my man. But woooooo I'm here to tell you that we are gonna have us some fun in this here bachelor pad of mine, Lightning Boy."

I look him square in the eyes. "Don't call me that."

He laughs. Clearly, he has no intention of stopping. "So, you been stuck out on the streets, huh?"

I nod.

"And wild Ariana happened to pick up your ass and pull you outta the gutter. Well, you are one lucky dude. That woman can get you the easiest money you ever made. I swear it. Think traveling to crazy-ass places. Getting your photo taken prancing down a runway. It's money for nothing. Worse thing is, you have to wait around a lot, but that's okay because you can always get your dick sucked while you're filing your nails and…" He trails off.

Smoke must be coming out of my nostrils or something.

"What? You don't like the sound of that? You hustled for cash out there, I'm guessing."

I grunt.

"Yeah, well that'd probably put anyone off blowjobs. Giving them, anyway. Maybe what you need is to receive a no strings attached one for a change. I'm willing to pay it forward if you're interested in a little stress relief. You look kinda wound tight."

I don't get it. Why does everyone want to do this shit with me? "No thanks. I'm not into guys."

He gives me a look that calls bullshit.

"I swear it."

"You're a *rent boy*. So how does the not liking guys thing work out for you in that profession?"

"Well I have to eat, and there are plenty of idiots happy enough to pay to shove their cocks in my mouth. So..." I give a lazy shrug so it looks like I'm not angry. "I just make sure it's over fast. That's why they call me Lightning."

"You fuck them?"

"I try not to. But sometimes... not very often and only for a helluva lot of money."

His smile mocks me. "Right. You don't like guys, but you miraculously get your dick hard enough to penetrate their un-sexy hairy bodies. Your story is not ringing true, my man. I think you might need to face facts and admit that you—"

"I can only do it if I hurt them," I say fast. I can't believe I've finally said it out loud. The ugly truth.

His eyebrows leap. "For real?"

"Yeah, man. Tie them to a chair and make the fuckers cry." There aren't too many chairs in public restrooms, but still. It's an idea for the future if things don't pan out with Ariana and this photo thing.

"Fuck. That shit turns you on?"

"Ah... no. Not in the traditional sense. Because... at the time, I'm not really thinking—*oh man I so wanna fuck you*. It's just... the thought of causing these shits pain has been known to get the blood flowing in the direction it needs to."

"Shit, man. You are one fucked-up dude. Someday, I want you to tell me exactly how you got that way."

Funny, I have a feeling that I just might.

His chin tips at me. "So, you on anything?"

Suddenly, his game controller has become the most fascinating item in the room. I study it, memorizing the buttons.

He waits. I stay silent.

Then he sighs, a bag of what I guess is junk food crinkling under his butt as he sags backward against the couch. "Right. Like that, is it? So you do the hard shit?"

I shrug. "Whatever I can get to ease the pain. Sometimes the harder the better, you know?"

Eyes bugging, he blows out a breath. "Well, you can forget about doing any of that garbage if you sign with Ariana. A bit of coke is fine. But nothing that will spoil the skin on your pretty face. Get it?"

"Sure. It's just a painkiller. That's all. If I'm comfortable, I won't need it." I don't think I will, anyway.

He gulps his drink, the sound loud and funny. *Bang* goes the bottle on the coffee table as he sets it down. "One more question about your fascinating sex-life."

Or lack thereof.

"Do you do girls?"

I bite my lip. Should I tell him? Completely beyond my control, my face scrunches up.

Angelo chuckles. "Well… spit it out. It's a simple question. Yes or no?"

"No."

Dreads swinging, his head pulls backward.

"I mean… I haven't done it with one… haven't, you know, fucked a girl. Uh… but sometimes I think about it, but then—"

"No way! You're not a pussy-virgin."

Why am I baring my soul to this nosy guy? I zip my lips.

"You are! You ain't never done no girl before. Shit, man.

You want me to fix you up? I know plenty of lovely ladies who'd be happy to help you get rid of your V card." He reaches for his cell. "Or should we call it a P.V. card?"

Before I can think it through, I launch myself at him, tearing the phone away.

"Hey!" he yells as I throw it across the room. "You've probably done gone and fucked it now, you caveman."

I lean forward and pull at my hair. The pain feels good. "Sorry. I just… I don't really do sex. It's complicated. Don't hassle me about it and we'll get along fine." I hope. Because I want to stay here. This place is the coolest, and he's a pretty funny guy.

Raising his palms, he says, "Peace, bro. No problem. You go crazy cranking your plank, and I'll leave you to it."

Instantly, my mind goes to sad-girl. My dick, too. I picture her body. Her face. I start to burn.

Need to get rid of Angelo fast.

I yawn loudly, and he laughs. "Tired, huh? I'll show you the spare room. And tomorrow I'm gonna give you the low down on this crazy modeling caper. After that, I'm gonna teach you how to cook a Jamaican curry and then, because this is even more important than good food, we are gonna game our asses off for twelve-hours straight."

"Wait." I shoot up, shaking my head as panic sets in. "I don't think I can—"

"What? Sit down," he interrupts. "You're not gonna stay?"

"No, man, I wanna stay. But, will it be okay if I sleep on the couch?"

He looks at me like the zombie apocalypse is upon us and

I've just come out of the closet as a flesh-eating freak.

"Why? The spare room is awesome. It's no trouble, I assure you."

"I bet it's a great room. But, I just can't handle too many doors between me and the outside."

"Worried I'm gonna lock you in and fatten you up so you taste better, Goldilocks? That's okay. I get where you're at."

I flop back on the soft, comfortable couch. "You know, I think that was Hansel and Gretel... the story with the cage and the food."

"Well, since you're so savvy with your fairy tales, Lightning Boy, you should be well aware that the handsome pauper-boy always turns out to be a prince. That's you. Things are looking up for you kid. You're safe. You can relax."

Safe?

I whisper the word, bite down on the sound as it breezes over my lips.

"Well, that'd be cool," I say, stretching my arms overhead. My back cracks loudly. "No one's ever helped me before so..."

His eyebrows twist. Maybe in shock. Or sympathy.

I throw back the rest of my beer and get to my woozy feet again. "Where's the bathroom?"

"How about a shower before you crash? Might help you sleep better if you feel a little less funky."

A shower. It's been a while. "You mean smell less funky."

"You said it, man. Come with me. Wait till you get a load of the six head shower contraption. It's fucking insane."

6

THE FUTURE

Angelo is right. The shower is fifty shades of fucking insane, the bathroom itself unearthly. I'm talking about a massive plunge pool set deep into a stepped stone platform, the scale and design fit for the king of the underworld.

The walls are metallic mosaic tiles of blue, green, and orange. Spooky lights shimmer through a huge round window like the damn thing is a portal to another universe. It probably just looks out over the bay. It's cool, though.

My head turns and turns as I take it all in. Okay, guess that crazy-ass looking alcove is the shower. Or a solarium. Or a teleportation device.

I strip off and fumble with knobs until I find the right lever. Water jets from fucking everywhere as I yank it. Then I step into the flow. Oh. Fucking. Hell. That's damn good. Light sparks off my wet skin while I gawk at the lavish surrounds, still unable to believe my change of luck.

This whole scene is surreal—just like that girl.

Water pummels me, the heat almost too much. It's shooting from no less than six different shiny heads that stick out from the walls. I've never felt anything so satisfying in my life.

Speaking of shiny heads and satisfaction…

I glance down at the one on the end of my hard dick. Jesus. Why did I allow myself to think of black-dress girl? If I obsess about her, I'll only end up feeling as sad and lonely as she looks.

In addition, empty, lost. And worthless.

But is she really sad and lonely?

And am I worthless?

Truth is, I probably won't lay eyes on her again and I'll never learn a thing about her. That's for the best. Because what would she want with a dirtbag like me, anyway?

I pump herbal smelling gel out of a ceramic bottle and soap up my chest. My dick pulses. I need to jerk off, get some relief, but with my legs this weak, I'll probably pass out when I come.

I wash every millimeter of skin until I smell like a flower farm—well not quite everywhere—I've saved the best bit for last. I should be able to stay upright as long as I don't let myself get off completely.

Head pressing back against the tiles and water gushing over my face, I slide my hand down my stomach. My heart pounds as I picture her, the curve of her hips, her dark eyes sifting through the shadows where I lurked. I give my cock a slow, torturous pump.

Then another.

It's hard to breathe.

Holding my base tightly, a groan vibrates through my chest. Blood throbs past my fingers, the veins of my dick pulsing. I'm so ready to sink into warm, wet, heat. That girl's body.

My legs shake as I start to get into it, using my other hand to bring my balls into the game. Fuck. I think I'm losing control, and my plan to stay conscious in this stupidly princely bathroom is evaporating with the steam. I'll hit the stone floor hard any minute. Hope I don't break anything.

Who cares. What would it be like to suck on sad-girl's lips? Those magnificent tits?

My breath comes in harsh pants, and I keep pumping, wondering what the girl smells like. Feels like. Then my leg muscles lock, my head spins, and I freeze. Not gonna *swoon* like some weakling loser. No way.

I picture her smile, the one she gave Cooper, and my hands drop to my thighs. Fucking Cooper. He's a buzz kill. I cradle my skull in my palm, fingernails digging in hard.

Thank Christ I thought of Cooper, because I am seriously close to passing out.

The lever that shuts down the deluge of water squeaks when I flick it. Then I dry off with a velvety towel, dick still leaping in pathetic pleas for attention. What a dumbass it is. I need to be on my back before I can attempt to deal with it—in bed where there's nowhere left to fall.

When my hair has stopped dripping, I take my raging erection back to the living room where Angelo has laid out a fluffy white duvet and a pillow. Fuck! *A real-life pillow.*

I scratch my head, calculating when I last used one of those foreign items—definitely another lifetime ago—and stare around the empty room, the luxury trappings taunting me with their exoticness.

This is a fantasy world.

When I open my eyes later, will I be hogtied and drugged and possibly have a knife sticking out of my gut? Who gives a fuck. That probably isn't gonna happen. But if it does, as least I'll be warm and hopefully unconscious while I wait.

Better lie down, then. I don't. Instead, I gaze at the cloud-soft covers for a while. What am I afraid of? That I'll be *too* comfortable? Or that I'll wake from this dream and be laid out next to the old railway, smelling like gutter water as usual?

I am officially a chickenshit.

Right, I'm just gonna get in.

The crisp cotton crinkles as I fold back the duvet thing and slip underneath.

Fuck, yeah.

Stretching my aching body, I huddle down, groaning like a wild creature in a trap. If this is death, then it's gonna be a very blissful time cocooned here waiting for the end. Pretty soon I'll be as hot as a furnace. Probably in more ways than one. Bring it on.

I pull the covers up to my neck. They smell like lemons. Ah, goddamn it, the standing lamp next to the fireplace is still blazing. That's okay—that fucker can stay burning. Then it might shine some light on the pretty rasta-dude when he comes for me with a kitchen knife, granting me some warning. *Fuck.* See how I can't let go of the idea?

Even with the amber lamp glowing, the dark still slithers toward me from the corners of the room. And I wait, feeling shut up, locked in, defenseless.

Ah, just go to sleep idiot. I should be used to this feeling. After all, ever since Mom died—it's how I grew up.

Always waiting in the dark. Shivering and shaking, fighting back nausea. Always wondering. Will it happen tonight? Is he coming for me again? Night after fucking night.

That voice from the past starts to whisper and snarl. I smack my fist into my temple hard, and I push the hated sound down deep. Nope. Nope. Nope. I won't let it wreck my first comfortable sleep in forever. Not fucking here. And not now.

Because, tonight I want to feel good. I'm gonna treat myself and for once let the lust simmering through my veins go all wild-fire and burn itself out.

Normally, being turned on brings bad, bad, feelings. Shame and hate. Disgust. Can't say I like it much. So, whenever I get myself off, I don't see any girl in particular. There's no whole person I'm getting into. It's just a hot-mess mix of imaginary body parts. Silky slopes and wet crevices—fashioned into how I guess the secret parts of a girl's body might look and feel.

Just like the havoc I unleash on the fuckwits in the park, I make sure it's quick, always get it over with fast. Because I'm Lightning Boy, right? Like Angelo said.

I don't dig the head space I get lost in when I'm train-wrecking toward the big-O station. Nope, I fucking hate it. The weakness. Disappearing into nothingness. It ain't safe. Not for me, anyway.

But, now, palm drifting down my hot skin, I think of the sad-eyed girl and let flames lick through my blood. It's shocking, because I feel far from annoyed by the situation. It's as if my past doesn't exist, and I can't wait to get into it. Crazy.

My dick feels heavy, hypersensitive, precum already seeping, and it couldn't get any harder.

Sad-girl's face—sweet and hot—is all I can see.

Then the dress, crushing her curves like a black bandage. I do the same to myself, squeeze hard, breathing loudly through four slow strokes.

My hands shake. My stomach feels like it's filled with vibrating feathers. Feathers made of cement. What? That doesn't even make sense. The feeling intensifies. Fuck, I might blow any second.

Shit. This is too fast. Not gonna let it happen yet.

My hands drop, fists twisting into the covers. The friction of the bedclothes will be enough to push me over. But that doesn't stop me moving against them, the slow rock of my hips agonizing.

Hands still clawed into linen, I transport myself back to Jackson Street, picture walking through the rain and strolling right on up to the girl.

Water hits my boots as I splash through puddles. I duck outta the way of a car, the screech of its horn loud at my back.

It feels and sounds and smells so real.

I've always had a superior fantasy life—needed one to survive. At this moment, I'm thankful for it.

So now here I am, apparently standing in front of her. And, fuck, she looks like the genuine article too. Good job brain. I should design robots. Or sex dolls.

I clear my throat and she looks up, her sexy, dark eyes widening. She takes a step away. Yeah, I probably look a mess, like some filthy, tattooed demon come to ravage. A fucking terrifying sight. Funny how in my fantasy I'm still unwashed, yet here I lie as clean and shiny as I've ever been.

"It's okay." I stretch a hand out, bridging the space between our bodies—only two feet, but it feels like an ocean. "Hey, don't be afraid. My name is Li—" Cutting me off, her hand zips out and twists into my t-shirt. Huh? I lose balance as she tugs me around a corner and shoves me backward, the brick wall grating my skin. "—Lightning," I finish. "My name is Lightning."

She smiles and fuck it's beautiful. Like a candle flame filling up a dark space, banishing every single ghost. We puff and pant at each other, staring and staring, and I'm lusting so bad for her body. To touch her.

It's not real.

It's not real.

I don't care. And it's a good thing that this is only happening in my head, because I've never done this before, so it won't matter if I fuck it up. This weird sound comes out of me as I lift both hands, slowly, slowly and then, *holy fuck*, I'm exploring her tits. Well, her fictional tits, but even so—it's a better high then anything I can buy out on the streets.

Horns beep in the distance. People yell. And I don't care about any of it.

Her eyelids flicker closed as I slip my clumsy paws into her dress, the skin silky beneath my fingertips. I drag the material below her breasts. Yep, my imagination is first-rate, because, Jesus, what a sight—dark nipples and round, soft flesh to caress and knead. I pull her in tight, wrap her in my arms, and crush her way too hard. Lucky she's not real.

She grinds against me, her head falling back. When her eyes open, they're not sad anymore, they're hot. Sparkling. Fiery.

Somehow, she's got her hands in my jeans, and she's stroking and massaging. Light then fast. Soft then hard.

"Lightning," she whispers. With a firm grasp on my wrist, she drags my hand down to her core, my palm scraping skin along the way. The black dress is hiked up around her waist and she's dripping *fucking* wet.

I pant and groan like I'm dying. Fuck any second I'm gonna come so hard… but no.

Not like this.

I shove her against the wall, grip myself, and push into her heat. *Oh, man.* She makes this guttural sound, and the feel of her—glove-tight—is freaking mind blowing.

I plunge in and out.

In.

And.

Out.

Long strokes.

Hard strokes.

And, fuck.

I don't know if a real-life girl would feel like this... but whatever... because this is *amazing*. Jerking off has never felt so good.

I heave her further up the wall and piston my hips in time with her moans.

"Fuck yes. Fuck yes," I say, my hand delving under the covers, pumping my dick frantically. Then I'm groaning and moaning like it's the end of the world. Everything winds tighter, coiling and spiraling. Up. Up. Up. I'm gonna...

Stop.

Stop.

In the alley, my hand grips her hair tight as I balance on the knife's edge, the rest of my body frozen. Don't move. Don't move.

It can't end.

Not ever.

"What's your name?" I ask, voice coming in panted bursts. I need to know. Then as she begins to speak, I fall and tumble over into oblivion.

"*No.* Fuck!" I can't hear her. I *need* to hear her, but I can't stop sinking—down, down, down—exploding like the mother of all fireworks until I hit the bottom.

Fuck.

I'm blind. Deaf. Defeated.

Gone.

Like her.

My eyes flare open. I'm crashed over the couch, my limbs shaking like jelly. There's no flame-eyed girl. No black dress. No smokin' hot body to hold on to. It's just me and my buzz saw breathing. And my hand covered in an impressive load of jizz.

Ah, shit. Angelo definitely *will* kill me when he sees what I've done to his cloud-like bed linen. It's not exactly heavenly anymore.

I spend a while wheezing like an asthmatic before I'm able to creep to the bathroom and wipe myself down. I grab a wad of toilet paper and try to do the same to the duvet. Then I collapse back into the warmth of my couch-bed, brain whirling with crazy thoughts.

This is what I want.

A house. A home. A place where I can dream about the girl in peace and safety. Not looking over my shoulder or hustling for food, feeling like shit all the time. I don't want to do that anymore.

If Ariana is for real and it's true that a guy like me can make good cash just by getting his photo taken, then I'm gonna learn how to do it right. For once in my life I plan to be good at something.

And fit in somewhere, be like every other guy who does the same shit for a living. Because I want normal. I want all this—everything Angelo has—so freaking badly.

I want to feel human.

To be a guy who just wants a girl.

No blowjobs, no hollow, painful gut. No stench and cold and dirt-shit loneliness. No Coop. No memories.

Just a guy. A guy who wants a girl.

I think of Cooper and the last time I saw him—back when I ran.

It wasn't so long ago. I was nearly seventeen. Now I'm eighteen.

So. Fucking. Young.

Shit. Yeah.

But eighteen—eighteen is just a number. Right?

Yeah, it's just a number.

Fucking *eighteen*.

Eighteen. Eighteen. It keeps looping around my head, driving me nuts. My brain is fracturing and seriously needs a full reboot.

I thump my skull into the pillow—it feels good—and I remember that it's all okay. It's fine because eighteen is only one way to live.

One way to fuck up.

To kill or be killed.

A way to ruin everything if I don't change.

But I won't be this young and stupid for long. I won't be that number. I'll be older. Steadier.

Strong.

When that day comes, Cooper better look the fuck out, because I'll be coming for him.

An uncomfortable feeling drops over me, smothering like a hot blanket.

It feels fluid. Wet. It's the past and the future and all my days colliding together into a sticky mess.

And I know. I know in my bones that time moves fast, like a river gushing by. Days will pass, nights too. Hopefully, they'll be easier than what I'm used to. And before too long, I'll be a man good and proper. A steady one. And, who knows, maybe even a fucking *rich* one.

That idea is hilarious.

Yeah, I'm not sure about that.

But I *will* be primed for revenge. Oh, yes, I'll be a loaded gun. Cocked and ready.

Closing my eyes, I summon the girl's image again, wishing for her. Wanting to know—maybe just once—what she feels like in reality. Not in a dream conjured up by lust. I draw her sad eyes close to mine. Imagine taking her hips in my hands, trapping them again, and pulling her in. Not letting go this time.

I'm hot inside, a treacly warmth spreading through my veins as I wish for this. Fucking pray for it.

And, of course, this makes me an idiot, because I've forgotten the warning—the one my mom gave me over and over when I was a kid.

Be careful what you wish for.

Be careful, my little lion.

My angel.

Be careful.

Because you just might get it.

And four years later…

I do.

I *fucking* get it.

7

EDEN - ONE HOUR LATER

"Did you enjoy your birthday, Eden?" Cooper asks as he pulls up outside my apartment block. He flicks on the car's interior light, beady eyes burning into mine.

Did I?

The restaurant was fancy, but I barely ate a thing.

Coop noticed and, like the control freak that he is, forced a bag of greasy fries down my gullet on our walk back through the seedy part of town. He loves to remind me where I'd be if it weren't for his so-called benevolence. Believe me, kind and caring this guy isn't.

Now where was I? Right. My eighteenth birthday…

All night, Coop had been edgy, sick plans and schemes clearly brewing beneath his furrowed brow.

The rain on Jackson Street was heavy. My mood gloomy.

So the truth is… no, I didn't enjoy my birthday.

But the smile currently stretched over my face tells a different story—the version I hope he'll swallow down without question. It's all gratitude and *oh-my-god-you're-the-best-guy-ever*. What crap. "Thank you," is the most I can force myself to actually say on the matter.

He looks pleased, the fool. "Good. You're only eighteen once. Live it up." The navy suit jacket strains as he pulls an expensive wallet out of his breast pocket. He's putting on weight. "I nearly forgot to give you your present."

Heaven forbid!

The wallet flips open and pudgy fingers dip and delve inside it. A creased photo lies across the middle. His thumb keeps it in place.

Who goes to the trouble of printing photos these days? I've unfortunately known Coop for two repulsive years now —far too long—and I've never seen this thing before.

"Who's that?" I ask, leaning a little closer. I hate the smell of his aftershave. Expensive. Overpowering.

His grin flickers as he flaps the photo between us. "An old friend." He chuckles like a slob. "Or should I say a *young* old friend."

Yuck, Coop is gross. "Can I see?"

Eyes narrowed, he studies me. My long brown hair in a wet tangle from the rain. Silly black dress, tight like a bandage. Dark red lips pretending to smile. I don't know why he looks so suspicious of my appearance, he made me like this.

After giving the picture a cherishing fondle, he hands it over.

I grip it hard, because Coop is likely to change his mind any moment and whip it away. He loves to power trip like that.

I look down at the photo. "Oh," I say as I press a shaking palm against my chest.

"Oh, indeed," he agrees.

A boy who could be my age sits on a couch. It's Coop's couch. Broad back to the camera, the guy wears jeans, swirls of intricate ink—and that's about it. Torso twisted, he looks through chunks of dirty blond hair over his shoulder, directly at the photographer. Or, in this case, the person viewing the image. Lucky me!

He's laughing but he doesn't look happy. Arrogance shapes scorn into every feature. Even his eyes—his *electric* blue eyes—are bitter and mocking as they hook me hard, drag me close, and ruin me.

I stutter in confusion. "God. This is... unbelievable. He's..."

"Oh. Yes." Coop snickers. "He most certainly is."

My heart pounds. "What's his name? How come you've never spoken about him before?"

"Thirteen months ago, I was negligent, and he slipped through my fingers. But I'm doing my best to remedy that stupid fucking mistake, Eden."

My blood chills at the violence in his eyes. Something else lurks in his expression. I'm not sure what it is, but icy shivers prickle over my skin from its intensity.

"Well, who is he?"

"Somebody that I used to know. And plan to again. Very

soon, I hope."

That poor guy. *I* hope he's well hidden. "Coop! You're not answering my question."

"You don't need to know, Eden. He's my little secret."

A dirty one, I bet.

As my fingers stroke the photo, Coop breathes a sleazy laugh through his nostrils. "Nice, huh?"

Nice is not the word for this face. The smile. Those eyes.

Something claws deep inside me, a sick longing, as I pass the picture back. "He's okay, I guess." Liar liar pants on fire.

Bushy eyebrows hike upward, his brow tightening as he digests my unexpected answer.

It's never wise to let Cooper know your attention has been snagged by anything. The guy lives to take things away from people.

In the light of the street lamp, rain streams down the car window in pretty orange rivulets. Preparing to head into the cold, I tug the annoying black dress down my thighs. My nipples will probably freeze and shatter the second I open the door.

Oh well, given my lack of prowess with the opposite sex, I doubt I'll ever have a need for them.

"Here." His disgusting paw goes to my shoulder, the other holding out a thick wad of notes. "Here's your present. Buy yourself some text books for school. I know they're probably the only luxury you'll allow yourself."

True.

I need to get qualified. I need work. And I need to pay Coop back and then never ever *ever* set eyes on him again.

I don't know much about life, about who I am or where I'm going, but one thing is certain—Cooper Martinez is a prick. I have to break free from him.

"Thanks," I say, tucking the money into my purse, already shuffling away from him.

I open the door, wobble onto the sidewalk, and then slam it shut without a word. I imagine his smug laugh as he pulls off the curb. And because he likes to take his time letting go, he drives slowly down my street.

I want to see the stars twinkle before I head upstairs, but the sky is overcast. Leaden. Like my heart.

I'm lonely. Lost. Like the boy in Coop's picture.

That guy makes my insides melt. My outsides quiver. My heart dance.

And as much as I'd like to lay eyes on him in the flesh, see that smile, touch that face, I hope with every part of my being that this boy stays hidden.

A slice of sky appears between a break in the smoky-gray cloud cover, a bright star shining down through it.

I make a wish. I say a prayer. I whisper a plea.

May that boy stay lost.

May he never be found.

Keep him safe.

Keep him safe.

The story continues four years later. Keep turning to read the blurb and a preview.

ABOUT BOOK 2 - LOVING L

Eden:

I only want one thing in life—and it isn't to be blackmailed into performing with a stranger for the entertainment of creepy voyeurs. But when dirty-copper Coop says jump—I ask how high.

The guy he sets me up with is nothing like I expect. He's so much worse.

Lightning. Beautiful as sin. Scary as hell. And, like me, he's damaged goods.

So now I want four things.
One. The deed to my dad's farm back.
Two. To know why a guy as gorgeous as L has never been with a girl before.
Three. Cooper to die a painful death.

And the last one starts with the letter L.

Previously titled Lightning Boy, Loving L is a full-length self-contained novel with a HEA.

Keep reading for a little preview…

AMY J. HEART
Loving
L
DAMAGED SOULS
GOLDEN HEARTS

LOVING L PREVIEW

Eden - Four years later

Before Sam died, he passed on two pieces of advice. One good and the other just plain weird.

The good: if your heart aches every single time you look at someone—run and run fast—because it probably won't end well. It sounded fair enough at the time, considering what he'd gone through with my mother. She left when I was three.

And the weird: lightning never strikes the same place twice. Sorry? Was that even true? I suspected a little Googling would shoot that one down fast, but I didn't pull out my cell to check. That would be a waste of time. And Dad didn't have much of that left.

Out of all the corny lines he could've chosen to pass on to his teenage daughter, those two were kind of lame. I longed for precious words I could hold close to my heart, pretty words that I could cling to over the years. So to be honest, I was disappointed.

"Remember those two things, Edie," he'd said, his bony fingers pinching my arm.

I nodded obediently and kissed his gaunt cheek. Then in the rundown cottage on our ramshackle lavender farm, I slumped over the bed, watching the cancer chomp away at his body, and decided that the disease must have finally reached his brain.

Why else would he waste his precious breath spouting mad theories about lightning?

After he'd fallen asleep, I called his oncologist. And within the fortnight, Dad was dead.

Then a whole six years later, it only took one meeting with a boy called L for me to realize that my father had been dead right, no pun intended, about the heartache bit. One look at that guy and he got under my skin, tore my heart out.

And not long after making L's acquaintance, I knew for sure that Dad had been wrong about the second thing—about lightning.

It *could* strike the same place twice. And the same person, too.

Repeatedly.

I was hard evidence, because that boy was Lightning with a capital L. And he blew me into pieces several times over.

And one horrible day, when I knew L a little better, I stared into his furious neon eyes that were way too close to mine, and all I could think was—why? Why the hell hadn't I run and run fast?

Just like Sam had told me to.

Eden

I hate Coop.

The sweaty, dead-eyed, sleazy-pig bastard. And this might seem a *little* over the top, but I wouldn't mind killing him one day.

I don't know when. Or how. He's an ex-cop, and a dirty one, too, so it won't be easy to achieve. But as I watch his name—appropriately saved as *The Devil*—flash across my phone screen, I fantasize the hell out of it. Picture wrapping my fingers around his filthy throat, wishing my hands would miraculously morph into giant, stronger ones.

But who am I kidding? When I watch bank commercials on TV, I cry.

So it probably won't be me who kills Coop, but one day he'll get what's coming to him. He makes life difficult for enough people. It's only a matter of time.

I've just finished swimming laps at the local pool and I'm tired. The last thing I want is his dreaded summoning call. It's been almost five months since he's asked me to do something vile, but even before I answer my cell, I know. I know it will be bad. I pick up anyway.

His gruff voice barks out instructions. I hang up before he's finished speaking, because small victories are better than none.

The gray walls close in on me as I stand limp in the middle of the change room with my heart thumping, the smell of chlorine burning my nose and the thought of what Coop wants me to do stinging my eyes.

Wake up Edie. Think of it as one more step closer to getting Sam's farm back. Your farm back.

A home—it's all I want.

So, I haul major ass across town to be there within the hour. Because that's what my Lord and Master wants.

Be there by four-thirty, Edie. Or else.

Since I have no intention of finding out what *'or else'* means, at exactly 4.30 p.m. on a sunny Friday afternoon, I find myself in the marble bathroom of a soulless city apartment, stripping down to my underwear with Coop's beady eyes running over me.

"Get a move on, Edie. He's like a fucking wild thing. Likely to bolt any minute. So I don't know how long he'll stick around for. And I really, *really* need to pull this one off." He gives me a foul wink and adds, "So to speak."

Once upon a time, Coop was handsome. You can see it there in his bone structure. But his broad, princely features have long been ruined, puffed out by excess booze and depraved living. I'm sure the black heart pounding in his chest doesn't do much for his complexion, either.

Eyes rolling, I shimmy out of my stockings and slip off a black stiletto heel, leaning a sweaty palm against the green-tiled wall. "Why are you so worried? The word going around is that you've got this guy on a very tight leash," I mutter, reaching for my second shoe.

I hate the things, love my biker boots and any item of clothing that adds a protective layer. Today, I've worn the come-fuck-me shoes because Coop believes that they help get the job done. Make it easier. Like a tool belt on a carpenter. But I can't stand them a second longer, so I try to sneak them off.

"Not entirely. He's a loose cannon this one." Coop's laugh echoes around the room. "Hey, leave those shoes on. He just might like 'em. Fuck knows what will get the bastard jacked up. You know, I don't think he even *can* get it up for a girl. He probably never has before."

"Shit, Cooper! What if he can't? You promised this would be one of the last times you'd make me do this. No matter what happens today, please tell me that you'll count this."

I wrench paper towel from the dispenser and pretend to work on my smoky eyeliner in the mirror. No way I'm crying in front of this asshole. "It won't be my fault if he can't do it. I showed up here just like you asked me, wearing these stupid clothes."

In a flash Coop has me squashed against the wall, his beer gut pushing into my stomach, stale breath hot in my face.

Beefy fingers squeeze my windpipe. "Mind your manners, you stupid little bitch, or you'll find out what the extremely unpleasant alternative to 'helping me out' like this is. I don't think you'll like it."

Suppressing a smug grin, he drops his hand and steps back. "If you fuck this up, we're all in trouble here, so shut up and listen to the deal."

He folds thick arms over his navy sports coat, leaning on

the door behind which his kinky buddies wait. "Out there in the living room are three suits and my boy L. Now when you get in that room, ignore the suits, don't even look at them. Just do whatever the fuck L says. He'll be ready for you. Mentally at least. And you'd better fucking hope you can inspire him physically. When you're done, come back in here. I'll be waiting."

"You're not watching?"

"Not today."

Praise be!

"Stop looking at me like I've kicked your frigging dog and get a move on, Edie."

Right. Wonderful. So, I simply have to turn on a guy who, according to Coop, bats exclusively for the other team. Shit. With my overly-abundant female attributes, I think I'm going to be at a distinct disadvantage.

Coop strokes a lock of my long hair, making sure to press his thumb over my nipple through the red bra as he pushes dark strands over my shoulder. "You're looking good, Edie."

I repress the urge to smack him. "Only my friends call me that. I'd prefer all you other assholes to call me Eden."

"Feisty today, aren't ya?"

Coop smirks as I shrug him off. I don't want to speak to him any more than I have to, but curiosity gets the better of me. "So what's he like, anyway?"

"Who? L?" Coop snickers. "He's broken. Angry. And a completely ruthless prick."

I snatch my brush from the vanity and drag it through my

hair briskly so Coop can't see the terror in my eyes. Hopefully, he's just trying to scare me.

"Do you mean the letter L? Now that's a stupid name. No mother calls a baby that."

"True. When he was a kid, he was called something else. But living out on the streets, he earned a different name." Raising a bushy, gray eyebrow, he pauses for dramatic effect. "You wanna know what he's called?"

I puff a loud breath through copious layers of lipstick. "I asked, didn't I?"

"Well, that boy out there answers to the name of Lightning."

I freeze, skin prickling as an image of Dad's face strobes over my brain. Shit. I don't want his memory polluted by Coop and his filth. The hairbrush feels like a brick in my palm as I set it down on the counter. "Lightning? Really?"

"Yep. But mostly, he just goes by L."

"Why is he called Lightning? I mean it's a pretty weird—"

"He got the name because the little cunt was flash-fast. At everything. Stealing your wallet. Running away. And most impressively at getting people off. He could make a guy come in his pants within seconds. And he doesn't mind making them suffer, either, which they love. Made him famous in our little circle of twisted money makers. Speaking of which, those suits out there have paid a great deal of money to watch L try to fuck you, so quit stalling and go make it happen."

Try?

God, these little sex-party setups of Coop's are disgusting, but this has to be the sickest yet. And the most dangerous.

What kind of a person pays money to watch a guy attempt the impossible anyway?

Well, I won't have to wonder about the brains behind this sick scheme for much longer. I'm about to walk through the door and meet him.

And this L person. The guy sounds like he'd rather have sex with a pillow than a girl trussed up in red lace. But he might enjoy making me cry. So that's awesome for him. Me? Not so much.

Hopefully, L has a first-class imagination. It might help him get the job done.

Luckily for me, my body responds even when my brain doesn't want it to, and that's both a curse and a saving grace. It certainly reduces the pain factor.

"Want a hit of coke?" says Coop. "Something stronger? Might help if this goes badly. I know exactly what L's capable of. How far he's prepared to go. And believe me, Eden, it could hurt."

"No, thanks." Not even the fear of what's waiting for me out there is enough to make me go down that path. In a couple of hours this will be over. And I'll be that much closer to freedom.

That is if *Lightning* can play his part.

Picturing the psychotic dandy that I'm about to go and rub myself against like a sad cat on heat—wiry, slim, maybe wearing a cape with the letter L on it—I take a big breath and push through the door. Then nearly fall flat on my barely-covered butt.

Hells bells!

Completely naked, a scowling blond god stands next to a padded bench, hands on his lean hips, inked biceps flexing, and his impressive package looking far from fired up.

He's the polar opposite of a foppish dude in a superhero getup and about the most beautiful creature I've ever laid eyes on. And shit he looks strong.

Well, if I die today, at least I'll have a spectacular view as he squeezes the life out of me.

That's something, I suppose.

End of Loving L excerpt…
Read the full-length HEA end of Eden and L's story now!

AMY J. HEART
Loving L
L
DAMAGED SOULS
GOLDEN HEARTS

OTHER BOOKS IN THE SERIES

Thank you for reading Finding E!

I write about golden-hearted girls and broken boys finding redemption. Damaged heroes are my favorite, be they ex-street boys, male models, rock stars, or fae princes.

Hugest hugs to Aubrey at A.T. Cover Designs for the awesome covers. You freaking nailed L, girl! XXX

Books in the series:

Loving L: A Dark Romance the full-length end to L and Eden's story. They've found each other! Can they also find a way to break free from Cooper and get their long-deserved happy-ever-after?

Tempting Ivy: A Younger Man Romance Nico and Ivy's story.

A cocky rocker. An older woman. Fated love was never meant to easy.

Saving South: A Rocker Romance

A hidden pregnancy. A sweetie wrapped in bad-boy rock star packaging. Will one bite of South be enough?

Swing by and say hello at:

BookBub

Facebook

amyjheart.com

Newsletter Sign Up here or on my website.

amyheartromance@gmail.com

And if you happen to love reading about cursed fae princes falling for mortal girls, check out my enemies to lovers fantasy romance series, the Black Blood Fae.

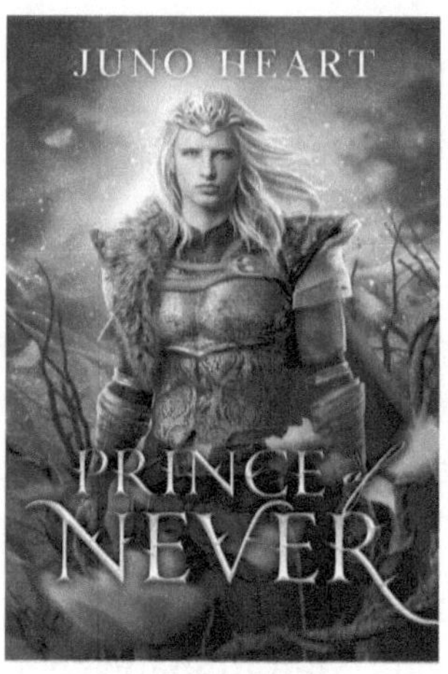

The Institute of Global Homelessness has excellent info about homelessness throughout the world.